'Yow!' Sam gave a violent start and stared at the slot near the top of the box. Laura looked at him. 'Stop it, Sam, will you? You nearly scared me to death. What's up with you?'

'There's . . . something inside the box, Laura.'

'I know, Sam. Letters.'

'No. No, it's something with eyes. I saw eyes.'

Laura gazed at the black slot. Her heart was pounding, but she wasn't going to let Sam see she was afraid. 'Well, there aren't any eyes there now,' she said.

'No – they went away when I yelled.'

'Rubbish. You're making it up, aren't you? To scare me.'

'No. No I'm not, Laura. Honest.'

She gazed at him. Even in the gathering gloom she could see that his face was white . . .

Nobody believes nine-year-old twins Sam and Laura when they tell them they've noticed something very odd about a postbox near the park. But Sam and Laura are determined to get to the bottom of the mystery – especially when Sam looks closer and sees something like a pair of eyes looking out of the box! Could something – or some*one* – be hiding in the postbox?

THE POSTBOX MYSTERY
ROBERT SWINDELLS

Illustrated by Jon Riley

YEARLING BOOKS

THE POSTBOX MYSTERY
A YEARLING BOOK 0 440 86275 2

First published in Great Britain by
Hodder and Stoughton Children's Books

PRINTING HISTORY
Hodder and Stoughton edition published 1988
Yearling edition published 1991
Yearling edition reprinted 1992, 1993

This book is set in 14/16 Century Schoolbook by
Chippendale Type Ltd., Otley, West Yorkshire

Yearling Books are published by Transworld Publishers Ltd.,
61–63 Uxbridge Road, Ealing, London W5 5SA,
in Australia by Transworld Publishers (Australia) Pty. Ltd.,
15–25 Helles Avenue, Moorebank, NSW 2170,
and in New Zealand by Transworld Publishers (N.Z.) Ltd.,
3 William Pickering Drive, Albany, Auckland.

Printed and bound in Great Britain by
Cox & Wyman Ltd., Reading, Berks.

*For Peanut, Queenie and Catherine,
with all my love*

Contents

1 How it Began 9
2 Eyes 17
3 Trouble at School 29
4 The Frightened Man 35
5 Trouble at Home 41
6 The Letter 47
7 A Light in the Sky 53
8 The Chase 63
9 How it Ended 75

Chapter 1

How it Began

Laura and Sam were nine-year-old twins. They lived with their dad on Elm Tree Avenue in Danby. They didn't have a mum, but that was all right because Dad was good at looking after them. He'd had plenty of practice, because their mum had gone away when the twins were only two.

Dad worked at an engineering factory called Parsons. He wasn't an engineer though. He was a security officer, which means he was responsible for seeing that doors and windows were securely locked and that the fence was in good repair. This was important, because the factory made machinery for drilling through very hard rock, and the only sort of drill which can do this is one with a diamond at its tip. There were always a great many diamonds at the factory, and if it hadn't been for Sam and Laura's dad, they'd probably have been stolen.

Dad went to work at half past seven, which meant that the twins had to get themselves ready for school and lock up the house. Locking

up was Laura's job – she was good at it, and meant to become a security officer herself someday. Sam's job was to clear the table, put the milk bottle out and check that the gas was turned off so that the house wouldn't burn down while they were gone.

Sometimes, the children had to do shopping on the way home from school. Other times they might tidy their rooms before Dad got in at five, and switch the immersion heater on for his bath. Managing without a mum had made Laura and Sam very sensible.

Laura liked school, but Sam didn't. Not usually, anyway. It was OK at the moment because they were doing a topic about the Royal Mail, and Miss Rogers had shown the class a Postman Pat video and taken them to see letters being sorted at the post office in the middle of town.

Today was Wednesday, and they were doing postboxes. There are different kinds of postboxes, and Miss

Rogers had big coloured pictures of them. She pointed to one and said, 'Who can tell me what this means?' She was pointing to some fancy lettering on the postbox. Danny Wilson put his hand up.

'Yes, Danny?'

'Please Miss, it's the Queen's initials.'

Miss Rogers smiled. 'Nearly right, Danny. What's our Queen's name?'

'Queen Elizabeth, Miss.'

'And what letter does Elizabeth begin with?'

'E, Miss.'

'And is this an E, Danny?'

'No Miss, it's a G.'

'That's right. So it's not the Queen's initial. It's King George's. King George the Sixth. He was king when our Queen was a little girl. And his father was king before him, and he was called George the Fifth. All the postboxes which were made in the reigns of the two Georges had this G on them, and we can still see lots of them today.' She pointed to a different picture. 'What's the initial on this one?'

Sam's hand went up. 'It's a V, Miss,

for Victoria. Queen Victoria, who lived a long time ago.'

'Very good, Sam. So, if we look for the initials on postboxes we find Vs, and Gs and Es. We don't find other initials, because it's been a very long time indeed since we had a monarch who wasn't a Victoria, an Edward, a George or an Elizabeth.'

Sam put his hand up again.

'What is it, Sam?'

'Please Miss, there's one with a C on it.'

Miss Rogers shook her head, smiling. 'No there isn't, Sam. It'll be a G which you've misread, or which has become damaged in some way.'

'No Miss, it's a C.'

'But that's impossible, Sam. Quite impossible.'

'Please Miss,' said Laura, 'it is a C. I've seen it too. It's on Prospect Street, Miss. Opposite Parsons, where our dad works.'

Miss Rogers shook her head again. 'I'll tell you what, Laura. Next time you and Sam are in Prospect Street, take a very close look at that postbox. A very close look. Then, if you still think it's got a C on it, you can take me to look at it one afternoon when school's over. All right?'

Laura nodded. 'Yes, Miss.'

Chapter 2

Eyes

At half past three, Laura and Sam decided they'd have a look at their special postbox on the way home. Prospect Street wasn't really on the way home, but there was no shopping to do so there'd be plenty of time to go the long way round.

'It *is* a C,' insisted Sam, as the pair left their friends behind and hurried through the little streets of Danby. 'I know,' said Laura. 'But Miss Rogers said we were to take a very close look and we will. Think how awful it'd be if we dragged her all the way to Prospect Street and it turned out we were mistaken.'

It was twenty to four by Laura's

17

watch as they turned the corner into Prospect Street. The postbox was at the far end, near the park gates, and Dad's factory was just across the road from it. The two children sometimes went into the park to snatch a quick go on the swings before running home, but that was in summer. It was nearly winter now, and the swings had been taken down. Besides, they had something more important to do. They hurried along by the park wall, anxious to get the job done and be home before dark. 'I hope Dad doesn't look out and see us,' said Laura. 'We'll cop it if he does.'

'There it is!' cried Sam, as the park gates loomed in the dusk.

'Course it is,' scoffed Laura. 'Did you think it might have run away or something?'

'Clever-clogs,' growled Sam, breaking into a run so as to get there first. He peered at the lettering and turned. 'It's a C, Laura, just like I said.'

'I said so too!' cried his twin. 'So there.' She came right up to the box and traced the outline of the letter with her finger. Then she put her face very close to it and screwed up her eyes and examined it.

'There's no damage,' she said. 'It's not a G with its curly bit knocked off. It's a C. Definitely. We can tell Miss Rogers we've—'

'Yow!' Sam gave a violent start and stared at the slot near the top of the box. Laura looked at him. 'Stop it, Sam, will you? You nearly scared me to death. What's up with you?'

'There's ... something inside the box, Laura.'

'I know, Sam. Letters.'

'No. No, it's something with eyes. I saw eyes.'

'Oh sure.' Laura's tone was scornful but she moved away from the box.

'Where? Where were these eyes then?'

'Th-there.' Sam's hand shook as he pointed. 'Where you put the letters in.'

Laura gazed at the black slot. Her heart was pounding, but she wasn't going to let Sam see she was afraid. 'Well, there aren't any eyes there now,' she said.

'No – they went away when I yelled.'

'Rubbish. You're making it up, aren't you? To scare me.'

'No. No I'm not, Laura. Honest.'

She gazed at him. Even in the gathering gloom she could see that his face was white. 'OK,' she whispered, taking hold of his arm and steering him further away from the box. 'So you saw eyes. Some animal's probably got in there – a cat or something – and it can't get out again.'

Sam shook his head without taking his eyes off the slot. 'I know cats' eyes, and this was no cat. It was bigger. There was part of a face.'

'An owl?'

He shook his head again. 'No. Not an owl either. Not any kind of animal. Something strange.'

Laura shivered. 'I suppose you're

going to tell me it was a ghost or a vampire or a skeleton or something, aren't you?'

'No. I'm not going to tell you anything, except there's something in there. I want to go home, Laura.'

'Wait. If there is something in the box, shouldn't we tell someone – the police or someone? I mean, if it's quite big it won't be able to get out, will it? It might die.'

'It'll get out when the postman comes to empty the box,' said Sam.

'It might jump out and scare him,' said Laura. 'It might even hurt him, Sam. I think we should tell somebody.'

'OK, but let's go, hey? If we see a policeman on the way we'll tell him, and if not we'll tell Dad. Right?'

Laura had to be content with that, and the twins set off home. They were nearly there when Laura spotted a policeman and a policewoman looking in a shop window. 'Hang on,' she said. 'I'll go over to tell them.'

'I wouldn't bother,' said Sam. 'Prospect Street's miles away, and besides, they'll never believe you.'

Laura shot him a suspicious glance.

'You didn't see anything at all, did you, Sam? You made it all up, and that's why you don't want me to tell them.'

'No, that's not why. I did see eyes. I did.'

'OK, then I'm going to tell them.' Her eyes glinted wickedly. 'Then, if you're lying, they'll take you away and lock you up and Dad and I will eat your fish fingers as well as ours.'

'Go on then. I don't care, because it isn't a lie. I'll wait for you here.'

Laura crossed the street. It was nearly dark. The two police officers were looking at rings in the brightly-lit window of a jeweller's shop. Laura went up to them.

'Excuse me.'

'Hmm?' The policeman turned.

'What's up, love – lost, are we?'

Laura shook her head. 'No. I want to report something.'

'Oh? And what might that be, Miss?'

'Something in a postbox,' said Laura. 'In Prospect Street.'

'What sort of something?'

'Something with eyes.'

'Oh yes? Something with eyes, in a postbox, in Prospect Street. See it yourself, did you?'

'No. My brother did.'

'And where's your brother now?'

'Over there.' She pointed.

The policewoman said, 'How old are you, love?'

'Nine. So's he. We're twins.'

'I see. And where do you live?'

'Three, Elm Tree Avenue.'

'Well, I think you ought to go home now, you and your brother. It's not a good idea to be wandering about in the dark, you know.'

'I know. What about the thing in the postbox?'

The officers exchanged glances, and the woman said, 'We'll look into it, love, don't worry. Straight home now, and don't get into anybody's car, right?'

'Right. Goodbye, then.'

'Goodbye.'

'What did they say?' demanded Sam, when she rejoined him.

'They said straight home, and not to get in anybody's car.'

'Didn't they believe you?'

'I don't know. The woman said they'd look into it.'

'Well, I hope they look into it and see something looking out.'

Laura laughed. 'Come on,' she said.

When Dad got in at five and Sam told him about the eyes, he laughed and said, 'You're having me on, old lad, aren't you?'

'No,' protested Sam. 'I'm not, Dad. Really I'm not. We told some police officers, and they said they'd look into it.'

'I think they were having you on, son. Did Laura see these eyes?'

Laura shook her head. 'But I believe Sam did, Dad. He looked as if he'd seen a ghost.'

'There's no such thing as ghosts, Laura.'

'I know that, Dad, but there was
something, I'm sure. We're taking
Miss Rogers tomorrow, because the
box has C-R on it.'

'G-R, you mean.'

'No – *C*-R.'

'That's impossible, love.'

'That's what Miss Rogers said.'

'Well, there you are then. Is the
water hot for my bath?'

Chapter 3

Trouble at School

As soon as Miss Rogers finished calling the register next morning, Laura put her hand up.

'What is it, Laura?'

'Please, Miss, we had a really close look at the postbox last night, and it is a C. Will you come and look at it today?'

The teacher looked thcughtful. 'It's very strange, Laura,' she said. 'I don't understand how there can possibly be a postbox with a C on it, but since you're so sure, I'll tell you what I'll do. I'll phone the post office at lunchtime, and if they can't give an explanation, I'll certainly come with you at hometime and look at it. We'll take the camera and get a snap of it for our topic book. How's that?'

'Thank you, Miss.'

At playtime Sam said, 'Why didn't you tell Miss Rogers about the eyes, Laura?'

Laura shook her head. 'Dad didn't believe us, and I don't think the police did either. If I told Miss Rogers, she'd probably think we'd made the whole thing up – the letter C as well as the eyes – and she wouldn't come and look.'

Sam looked crestfallen. 'You don't believe me either, do you?'

'Course I do, Sam, but grown-ups are different. They never believe anything kids tell them. We'll show her the C, and then we'll tell her about the eyes. OK?'

Just before the bell went for afternoon school, Miss Rogers sent for Laura and Sam to see her in the classroom. They hurried in feeling very excited, but Miss Rogers looked cross.

'Somebody's been telling me fibs,' she said sternly. 'I've just phoned the post office, and they tell me there is no postbox in Prospect Street.'

The twins looked at her with their mouths open. 'Well?' she said. 'What have you to say for yourselves?'

'But there is, Miss,' cried Laura. 'We saw it last night. I touched it.'

'And I saw two eyes looking out of the slot,' said Sam.

Miss Rogers frowned at him. 'That's another fib, Sam Webster,'

31

she snapped. 'I don't know what's got into you two all of a sudden – you're usually so sensible – but whatever it is, it's got to stop right now. Do you understand?'

'But Miss—'

'Right now, Sam.'

'Yes, Miss.'

Outside, Sam started to cry. 'Nobody believes me,' he sniffled. 'Not even you.'

Laura sighed. 'Oh, Sam,' she said. 'I told you not to mention the eyes, didn't I? I said it'd stop Miss Rogers coming with us and now she thinks there's no box at all. Here.' She thrust a tissue into Sam's hand. 'For goodness sake stop blubbing and blow your nose. We've got to think what to do.'

'What can we do?' sniffed Sam. 'The post office says there's no box. Why would they say that, Laura?'

'I don't know. They made a mistake, I expect. I wish we'd never mentioned

the box to Miss Rogers. Now she
thinks we're silly little fibbers and it
isn't fair. We've got to do something,
Sam. I'll have a think and let you
know at hometime. OK?'

'OK,' murmured Sam, as the bell
rang.

Chapter 4

The Frightened Man

'I think,' said Laura, as the twins walked home that afternoon, 'that we should have another look at that postbox. I want to see those eyes.'

'What if you don't see them?' asked Sam. 'What if the thing inside knows we're watching, and stays hidden?'

'It won't know we're watching, Sam, because it's us who'll be hidden. In the bushes, just inside the park.'

'When?'

'Now. What's wrong with now?'

'What about shopping? We have to get tuna and salad and stuff for tea.'

'If we hurry, we can do that and then go to the park. It'll be nearly dark then, and there'll be more chance of the thing showing itself.'

'What if it's not there any more? What if it got out when the postman opened the door?'

'Oh, what if, what if, what if!' cried Laura. 'We can try, Sam. It's all we can do.'

They rushed round the supermarket, then they were off, pelting along the road with plastic carriers bumping their legs. When the park gates came in sight, they slowed down.

'Right,' said Laura. 'I think we should creep quietly up to the gates, in case the thing looks out and spots us. We'll get behind the wall and hide in the bushes by the gate. Come on.'

They slid behind the gate and hid in the cover of the dark rhododendrons, right up against one of the stone pillars of the gateway. Here, they put their carriers down and peered out at the postbox.

'You can only see half the slot from here,' Sam whispered.

'Can't be helped,' hissed Laura. 'We'll see anything that tries to look out.'

For a long time, nothing happened.

It was November, and the twins' feet and hands grew cold. Except for the occasional car, the only sound was the drip, drip of water falling from the rhododendrons on to the sodden ground. Sam looked at his watch.

'Twenty-five past four,' he whispered. 'We'll have to go soon or Dad will be home before us.'

'Five more minutes,' Laura replied. 'It's nearly too dark to see now, anyway.'

They peered, half-frozen, through the gathering twilight. A car approached, slowing. Its headlights swept the rhododendrons and the twins drew back. The car pulled into the kerb and stopped. A man got out, leaving the engine running, and walked round the front of the vehicle with a small package in his hand. He approached the postbox, and was about to push the package into the slot when he uttered a sharp cry,

snatched back his hand and backed
away from the box with a frightened
expression on his face. As the children watched, he moved rapidly

round the car, got in, slammed the door and drove off at high speed.

'There!' hissed Sam. 'He saw them too, Laura. Now do you believe me?'

Chapter 5

Trouble at Home

When Dad walked in, there was more trouble. 'What were you two doing in the park at half past four?' he asked.

'Park?' said Sam, as though he didn't know what the word meant.

'Yes,' said Dad sternly. 'P-A-R-K park. And don't tell me you weren't there, because I saw you.'

'We were watching the postbox,' admitted Sam. 'You know – the one with the eyes.'

'Eyes?' cried Dad. 'I'll give you eyes, young man. How many times have I told you to stay away from dark, lonely places in the evenings? How many times have I said it's dangerous for young children to be messing around in parks and alleyways and badly lit streets at night?'

'It was only half past four, Dad,' protested Laura.

'It doesn't matter. It was dark, Laura, and children have been known to disappear at half past four in the afternoon, even in broad daylight.'

42

'We're sorry, Dad,' said Sam. 'But we had to do it. We told Miss Rogers about the C and the eyes, and she didn't believe us. She said we were fibbing and told us off.'

'I should just think she did!' Dad retorted. 'If I'd told a story like that to my teacher I'd have got the cane. You've got over-developed imaginations, the pair of you, and it's time you started behaving a bit more sensibly.'

Laura thought that was unfair. She was a lot more sensible than most of her friends, and so was Sam. There were not many children who shopped and cooked and had the house key and everything, but she couldn't say that to Dad. He made them both promise to stay away from the park after school, and went upstairs for his bath.

'What do we do now?' demanded Sam. 'We've promised.'

'I don't know,' growled Laura. 'We'll just have to forget about the postbox, I suppose.'

43

'I know one thing we could do,' said Sam.

'What?'

'Take a photo of the box.'

'There's just one snag about that idea,' said Laura.

'What's that?'

'We haven't got a camera.'

'Dad's got one.'

'Oh, great! Are you going to go up to Dad and say: Can we borrow your hundred-and-twenty pound camera so we can go to the park we've just promised to stay away from and get a shot of the postbox that isn't there – the one with the imaginary monster inside! Can you guess what he'd say?'

'Hey, just a minute,' whispered Sam, with a thoughtful look on his face.

'What?'

'We haven't told Dad the full story, Laura. He doesn't know the post office says there's no box. He knows there's a box because he can see it from the factory. If we could get him

44

to tell Miss Rogers that, it'd be something, wouldn't it?'

'It'd be a start,' admitted Laura. 'But I don't know whether I dare mention it to him. You know what he's like when he's mad.'

'Wait till he's eaten his meal. He'll be in a better mood then.'

Laura considered this as she put the potatoes to bake in the microwave. 'All right,' she said, closing the door and jabbing the button. 'I will.' She stood, watching the reflection of her face in the dark glass, while the potatoes went round and round like kids on a fairground ride.

Chapter 6
The Letter

'I've got more important things to think about,' said Dad, pushing away his empty pudding plate, 'than writing notes to teachers about postboxes. There's a big order in at work, and we're expecting an extra-large consignment of diamonds in the next few days. I'm going to be very busy making sure nothing happens to them, and I'm afraid you'll just have to sort out this spot of bother yourselves.'

'Does that mean,' said Sam, when Dad had left the room, 'that we can go to the postbox after all?'

'I don't think so,' said Laura.

'Well, how can we sort it out if we don't?'

'I don't know, Sam. I don't want to talk about it just now.'

They didn't talk about it any more until Saturday. Dad usually had Saturdays off work, and he'd take the twins out somewhere in the car. This Saturday was to be different.

'Those diamonds will be in tomorrow,' Dad had said on Friday evening. 'I have to be there when they arrive, so I'm afraid our outing's off.'

'Aw, flipping heck!' moaned Sam. His father frowned at him.

'You were taking us to the zoo,' said Laura. 'Can we go by ourselves, Dad – on the bus?'

'No, Laura, you cannot. You're far too young to be travelling twenty miles by yourselves, and besides, they don't let children in without an adult. You'll have to amuse yourselves with TV or play in the park.'

When Dad had left on Saturday

morning, and the twins were doing the breakfast things, Sam said, 'We could keep watch on the postbox all day today if we wanted.'

'Hmm,' grunted Laura. 'I don't fancy it, Sam. Have you seen the weather?' She hung up the tea-towel and went off to watch *Dogtanian*.

Sam lifted a corner of the curtain and looked out. There was a heavy mist, and it was drizzling.

'I'm going anyway,' he growled, getting into his anorak.

'Then we'll both be watching the box, sort of,' murmured Laura, her eyes on the screen. As Sam was leaving the room she said, 'Hey – just a sec – I've had an idea.' She got up and left the room, returning a moment later with an envelope and a ball-point.

'What're you doing?' Sam asked.

'Writing myself a letter.' She wrote her name and address on the envelope, sealed it and found a stamp

to stick on it. 'There.' She handed it to her twin.

'You're crazy,' he said. 'It's an empty envelope.'

'Ah-ha.' His sister nodded. 'You post that in our special box. If it's delivered here Monday, it means the post office knows about the box, and the person Miss Rogers spoke to made a mistake. If it isn't delivered, we complain at the post office and they'll have to investigate.' She grinned. 'We might even get a reward for reminding them about this forgotten postbox which they haven't emptied in years.'

'OK,' said Sam, 'I'll post it, but only if the eyes aren't there. And even then I'll shove it in and run before it grabs my hand and pulls me through the slot.'

Laura giggled. 'Perhaps we should stick a stamp on you, just in case.'

'Fun-nee,' said Sam, but he wasn't laughing.

Chapter 7

A Light in the Sky

It was miserable in the park. The bushes formed a canopy over his head and kept off some of the rain, but they made it dark and they didn't keep out the cold. There was nobody about, and Sam felt uneasy and bored. 'I'm fed up,' he told himself, looking at his watch. 'Ten o'clock. I'm sure it was ten the last time I looked. One more hour,' he promised himself, 'and if nothing's happened then, I'm off.'

Presently he heard the rumble of a heavy motor. He peered out. An armoured truck came nosing out of the mist with its fog-lights on. Its

flasher winked, and it swung in at the factory gate opposite. 'Diamonds!' breathed Sam. 'I bet there's a million pounds worth in that truck.'

He didn't see what happened after that because of the mist, but he heard the engine stop, and there were voices and some banging. After a quarter of an hour he heard the engine again and the truck came out, dazzling him with its fog-lights as it swung left and disappeared.

Nothing happened after that until ten to eleven, when Sam heard footsteps in the mist and saw somebody crossing the road towards him. 'Oh, heck!' he whispered. 'It's Dad. I bet he's spotted me with his x-ray eyes.' He shrank back into the rhododendrons and kept very still.

He needn't have worried. His father hadn't seen him. Sam watched as he walked round the postbox, bending to read the lettering and peering into the slot.

'Come on, eyes,' he breathed. 'Have a squint at my dad and everything'll be OK.'

The eyes didn't oblige, and after a minute Sam's father turned and walked back into the mist.

Sam sighed. 'Ah, well – at least he knows there is a box, and that it has a C on it. Time to go home, I think.' He'd just started to make his way back through the tangle when he heard a faint humming sound. Peering through the dripping foliage he saw a fuzzy pink light in the sky. He stopped. The light hung motionless for a moment, then sank slowly till it disappeared behind some trees in the middle of the park.

'The sun,' Sam told himself, though his heart was racing. 'It's the sun, setting at lunchtime and humming to itself like it sometimes does when there's nobody about.' He stood, gazing towards the trees. He was shivering, and not only with the cold.

'Who am I fooling?' he whispered. 'Let's go and take a look.'

Sam had barely begun moving in the direction of the humming when he heard the swish of wet leaves and the snap of a twig. Someone else was under the rhododendrons, coming towards him. He glanced about, spotted a particularly dense clump of foliage and squatted behind it, screwing up his eyes to see who or what was with him in this dim green place. The footfalls came closer, and some words flashed through Sam's mind from something he'd watched on television – *Something wicked this way comes*. He moaned softly, wishing he'd stayed home with Laura.

There were two of them. They came furtively, crouching along one behind the other, and Sam crammed his fist in his mouth to keep from screaming.

They passed within a metre of him, and there was no possibility of a

mistake. Massive heads they had,
and silvery faces, in the dark beneath
the trees. Sam bit his knuckles till
they passed, and when they were
shadows in the mist he rose silently
and followed.

At the edge of the trees they

turned, and followed the wall along
to the gates. Sam stayed well behind,
a shadow in the shadows. In the gateway they stopped, and Sam stopped
too. He saw them peer along the
silent road, first one way, then the
other. He saw how they darted across

the wet flagstones to the postbox, and how its door swung open, and how they clambered inside, one behind the other. He heard the click as the door closed, and then there was only the hiss of drizzle and the humming through the trees.

He stood watching the box. He was frightened – far more frightened than he had ever been in his life, and he didn't know what to do. He wanted to run into the factory and tell Dad what he'd seen, but he knew he couldn't. 'Who'd believe me?' he whispered. 'Who'll believe me now?'

Laura. She'd believe him. He'd run home and tell Laura, and perhaps she'd know what to do. And even if she didn't, he'd be safe. Safe and warm and dry.

He tiptoed to the gates, watching the box, and as he did so the humming grew a little louder. He turned. A fuzzy pink ball rose slowly from behind the trees. It hovered for a moment, then shot straight up with incredible speed and vanished, leaving a green, floating blob before his eyes.

Chapter 8

The Chase

'I believe you, Sam,' said Laura. 'Only don't say anything to Dad. Not yet.'

'When, then?'

'Monday. He'll be busy worrying about those diamonds right now, and besides, I want to see if that letter comes before we bring the subject up again.'

'It won't. I told you – nobody emptied the box.'

'They might have, after you left.'

'No chance. There's three monsters in there, Laura. From a spaceship.'

'You don't know it was a spaceship.'

'What was it then – a box of choc-
olates?'

'I don't know. Let's just leave it till
Monday, OK? Then we can go to the
post office and find out what's going
on.'

'What if Dad mentions the letter C
– he's seen it, you know.'

'There you go again – what if, what
if, what if. Just don't mention little
silver men, that's all.'

When Dad got in at half past four,
the first thing he said was, 'You kids
were right. I took a look at your
postbox today and there is a C on it.
I'm going to phone the post office on
Monday morning, and then I'll call
your teacher.' He grinned at Sam. 'I
didn't see any eyes, though.'

Sam opened his mouth to reply, but
Laura frowned and he shut it again.
Dad went off to his bath, and when he
came down he said, 'We had to miss
the zoo today, so I'm taking you
tomorrow instead.'

'Ooh, great!' cried Laura. 'But what about the diamonds?'

Dad laughed. 'Safely tucked away, love, in the underground vault, with a watchman on patrol. We can afford to forget about them until Monday.'

As they were to make an early start for the zoo, Dad sent the twins off to bed at eight o'clock. 'Straight to sleep, mind,' he said. 'No reading under the covers.'

Laura was soon asleep, but Sam lay thinking about pink lights and silvery faces, and it was a long time before he dropped off. When he did sleep, he dreamt Miss Rogers was dragging him towards the open door of a postbox. The postbox was in the classroom and when he looked at Miss Rogers's face it was a silver mask. He woke with a cry and heard the telephone ringing and footfalls on the stairs.

He sat up, knuckled his eyes and peered at the clock radio on his bedside locker – 4.59. Who on earth was ringing at five in the morning? He slipped out of bed and tiptoed to the landing. Laura was on the stairs. Sam joined her.

'Who is it?' he yawned.

'Dunno,' mumbled Laura. 'Dad's gone down.'

The ringing stopped as Dad picked up the receiver. They heard him say, 'Danby 4297,' in a grumpy voice. There was a pause, then he said, 'What? When?' very loudly. Another pause, followed by some words they didn't catch, and then the phone went down and Dad appeared, bounding up the stairs two at a time.

'What is it, Dad – what's up?' asked Laura. Dad brushed past her, heading for his room.

'The diamonds,' he rapped, as the twins followed him. 'The watchman heard a noise and went down to investigate. Somebody's tunnelled in. Cleaned out the vault. Got to get down there.' He snatched a coat from his wardrobe, pulled it on over his pyjamas, and stepped into his shoes. 'You kids go back to bed and I'll call you later, OK?'

'Just a minute, Dad.' Laura grabbed his sleeve. 'Where does the tunnel lead?'

Dad shook his head. 'Can't tell. They brought down the roof when they left. Blocked it off. Why d'you ask?'

'Because I think I know where it leads.'

'What d'you mean, Laura? How could you possibly know?'

'The postbox. I bet it leads to the postbox.'

'Look, Laura, this is no time to be—' He broke off, looking at her with an odd expression. 'Go on – what were you going to say?'

'Sam was watching the box today. Two creatures – aliens, we think they were – went inside. It's right opposite the factory, the post office knows nothing about it, and it's got the wrong initial on it. Don't you see, Dad – it may not be a real postbox at all. Perhaps the aliens were after the diamonds, and the box is a dummy covering the entrance to their tunnel!'

Dad gazed at Laura for a moment. 'Good Lord!' he whispered. 'You could

easily be right, you know. Why didn't
I – come on!'

The sky was still dark as Dad
reversed the car out of the drive. Sam
and Laura, anoraks over their night-
clothes, huddled in the back seat,
trying to keep warm. Dad drove
quickly through the deserted streets,
and as he drove he fired questions at
them in a grim, urgent voice. 'These

– aliens. Where did they come from – which direction, I mean?'

'The park,' Sam told him. 'There was a humming noise and a pink light in the sky. It came down in the park. A minute later the two aliens came through the bushes. I hid, and they went straight past me, as close as you are now. I saw them go into the box.'

'Why didn't you tell me, Sam?'

'Because . . .' Sam looked at Laura.

'I told him not to, Dad,' said Laura. 'Because you didn't believe us before.'

'Ah.' Dad nodded. 'It seems I might have been wrong there, Laura.' He glanced at Sam. 'Where, in the park?'

'The playing field, I think – behind the tall trees. That's where the light went down.'

'Right.'

Dad spun the wheel and the car turned, squealing, into Prospect Street. Its headlights swept across two police cars parked by the factory gate, then fell on the postbox. Sam cried out and pointed.

'What is it?' snapped Dad. 'I don't see anything.'

'They were there!' yelled Sam. 'Three of them, I think. They ran when the light hit the box.'

'Then we just might be in time. Hold tight!'

With a screech of tyres, the car swerved across the road, mounted the pavement and jerked to a stop centimetres from the park gates. Dad flung his door open and dived out. 'Come on!'

They followed him through the gates, through the rhododendrons, and over lawns and flowerbeds towards the trees. The light was just enough to reveal a number of small, ungainly figures, sixty or seventy metres ahead, running clumsily and in evident panic. As their pursuers gained on them, the aliens began throwing down the packages they were carrying, so that Laura and the others had to swerve and leap to keep from tripping over them.

'The diamonds!' cried Dad. 'They're dumping the diamonds.'

The aliens ran through the belt of trees and out on to the playing field with their pursuers close behind.

Laura looked up and gasped to see the thing that stood there. It was taller than a house. Lights of many colours rippled and pulsated along its flank and the sound that came out of it was like bees inside her skull. She saw it for only an instant, then screamed and flung up her arms as brilliant white light burst from the craft, blinding her. She sank to her knees with her arms wrapped round her head that had a million bees in it, and when she looked again there was only a scatter of packages on the grass and a light in the sky, receding.

Chapter 9

How it Ended

A week had gone by, and the twins had finally made it to the zoo. It was a warm day for November, and they were sitting on the grass with their father, eating a picnic lunch.

'What a smashing week it's been,' said Sam. 'Our pictures in the paper, letters of thanks from the post office and the police, an assembly about us at school, a reward from Parsons, and now this!'

Dad smiled. 'You deserve it, the pair of you. If it wasn't for you, those diamonds would be goodness knows where by now, and I'd probably be looking for a job.'

'I wonder where the aliens were

from, and why they came all this way for diamonds,' mused Laura.

'I reckon they were from a world that has no diamonds left, and they needed some – maybe to make drills as we do.'

'Maybe they eat diamonds,' said Sam.

Dad laughed. 'They'd need mighty ⸱trong teeth, old lad.'

'It was clever of them, though,' said Laura, 'to use a postbox as they did. Nobody notices postboxes – we wouldn't have if we hadn't been doing a topic about the post.'

'They weren't as clever as you two,' said Dad. 'You'd have put a V or a G or an E on the box, not a C.'

'I've just thought of something,' said Laura. 'If they'd waited till Sam and I were grown up, they'd have got away with it.'

Dad looked at her. 'Why's that, Laura?'

'Well,' she smiled. 'When Sam and I are grown up, Prince Charles will be king, and there'll be lots of post-boxes with C on them.'

'Laura,' said Dad, 'you're a genius.'

Laura wrinkled up her nose at him and stood up. 'Come on, Sam,' she said. 'Let's feed the birds.'

THE END

ABOUT THE AUTHOR

Robert Swindells left school at fifteen and worked as a copyholder on a local newspaper. At seventeen he joined the RAF for three years, two of which he served in Germany. He then worked as a clerk, an engineer, and a printer before training and working as a teacher. He is now a full-time writer and lives on the Yorkshire moors.

He has written many books for young readers, including the winner of the 1990 Children's Book Award, *Room 13* and *Dracula's Castle* (Doubleday and Yearling paperback), *Hydra* (published by Doubleday and a forthcoming Yearling paperback) and, for older readers, the award-winning *Brother in the Land* and *Staying Up* (published by Corgi Freeway Books). As well as writing, Robert Swindells enjoys keeping fit, travelling and reading.

A SELECTED LIST OF TITLES AVAILABLE
FROM YEARLING BOOKS

THE PRICES SHOWN BELOW WERE CORRECT AT THE TIME OF GOING TO PRESS. HOWEVER TRANSWORLD PUBLISHERS RESERVE THE RIGHT TO SHOW NEW RETAIL PRICES ON COVERS WHICH MAY DIFFER FROM THOSE PREVIOUSLY ADVERTISED IN THE TEXT OR ELSEWHERE.

☐	86212 4	**SAM, THE GIRL DETECTIVE**	*Tony Bradman*	£2.50
☐	86309 0	**SAM, THE GIRL DETECTIVE: THE SECRET OF THE SEVENTH CANDLE**	*Tony Bradman*	£2.99
☐	86273 6	**STAYING NINE**	*Pam Conrad*	£2.50
☐	86204 3	**CHARLIE COPPINS**	*Neville Crine*	£1.99
☐	86200 0	**FOG LANE SCHOOL AND THE GREAT RACING CAR DISASTER**	*John Cunliffe*	£2.50
☐	86290 6	**TOM'S SAUSAGE LION**	*Michael Morpurgo*	£2.50
☐	86264 7	**ATTILA THE HEN**	*Paddy Mounter*	£2.50
☐	86265 5	**POOR BADGER**	*K. M. Peyton*	£2.50
☐	86227 2	**ROOM 13**	*Robert Swindells*	£2.99
☐	86275 2	**THE POSTBOX MYSTERY**	*Robert Swindells*	£2.50
☐	86205 1	**JUMPING JACK**	*David Wiseman*	£2.50
☐	86201 9	**THE CREATURE IN THE DARK**	*Robert Westall*	£2.50

All Yearling Books are available at your bookshop or newsagent, or can be ordered from the following address:

Transworld Publishers Ltd,
Cash Sales Department,
PO Box 11, Falmouth, Cornwall TR10 9EN

Please send a cheque or postal order (no currency) and allow £1.00 for postage and packing for one book, an additional 50p for a second book, and an additional 30p for each subsequent book ordered to a maximum charge of £3.00 if ordering seven or more books.

Overseas customers, including Eire, please allow £2.00 for postage and packing for the first book, an additional £1.00 for a second book, and an additional 50p for each subsequent title ordered.

NAME: ....

ADDRESS: ....

....